# Count with The Very Hungry Caterpillar
## An Eric Carle Sticker Book

WORLD OF ERIC CARLE
An imprint of Penguin Random House LLC, New York

*The Very Hungry Caterpillar* originally published by Philomel Books, an imprint of Penguin Random House LLC, New York, 1969 and 1987

This edition published by World of Eric Carle, an imprint of Penguin Random House LLC, New York, 2019

Sticker Book Edition copyright © 2006 by Penguin Random House LLC

To find out more about Eric Carle and his books, please visit eric-carle.com.
To learn about The Eric Carle Museum of Picture Book Art, please visit carlemuseum.org.

Visit us online at penguinrandomhouse.com.

Manufactured in China

ISBN 9780448444208

15 14 13 12 11 10

In the light of the moon

a little egg lay on a leaf.

One Sunday morning the warm sun came up and—pop!—out of the egg came a tiny and very hungry caterpillar.

He started looking for some food.

On Monday he ate through one apple.
But he was still hungry.

 On Tuesday he ate through two pears,
but he was still hungry.

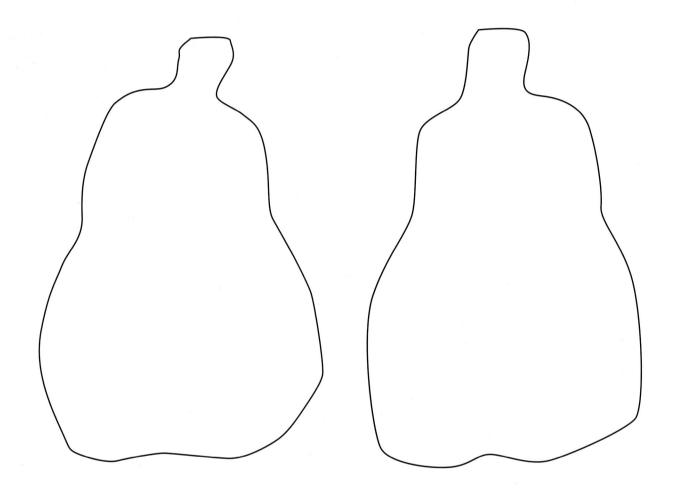

8

On Wednesday he ate through
three plums, but he was still hungry.

9

On Thursday he ate through four strawberries, but he was still hungry.

On Friday he ate through five oranges, but he was still hungry.

On Saturday he ate through one piece
of chocolate cake, one ice-cream cone,
one pickle, one slice of Swiss cheese,

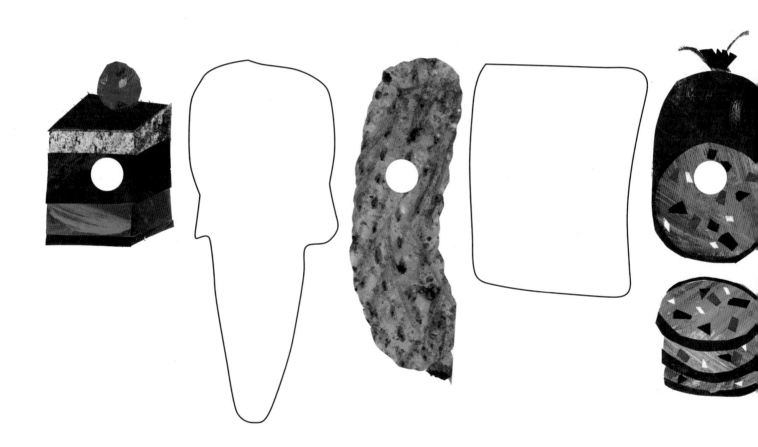

one slice of salami, one lollipop, one piece of cherry pie, one sausage, one cupcake, and one slice of watermelon.

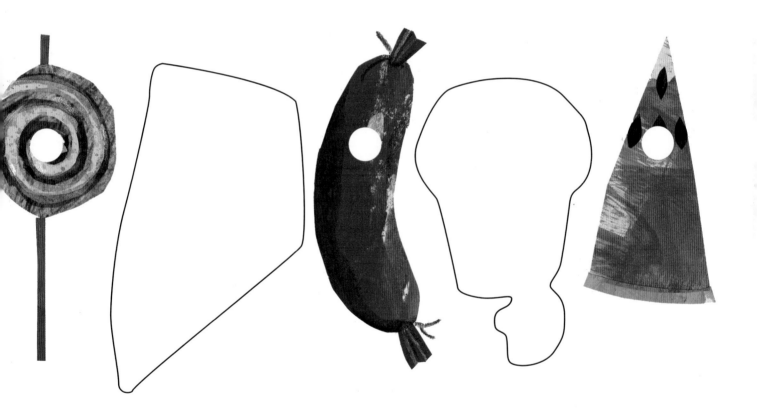

That night he had a stomachache!

The next day was Sunday again. The caterpillar ate through one nice green leaf, and after that he felt much better.

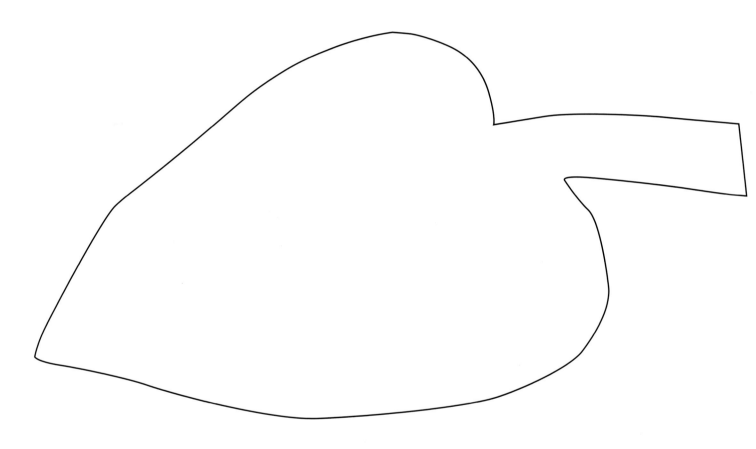

Now he wasn't hungry any more—and he wasn't a little caterpillar any more. He was a big, fat caterpillar.

He built a small house, called a cocoon, around himself. He stayed inside for more than two weeks.

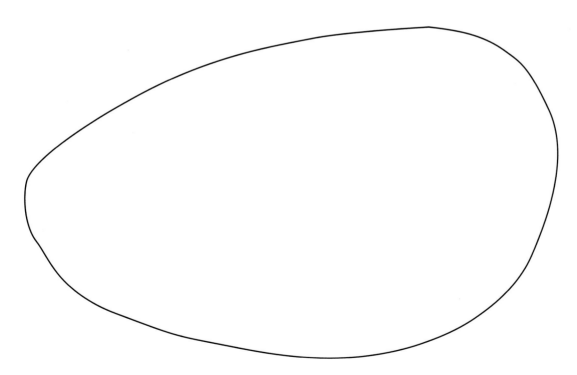

Then he nibbled a hole in the cocoon, pushed his way out and . . .

he was a beautiful butterfly!

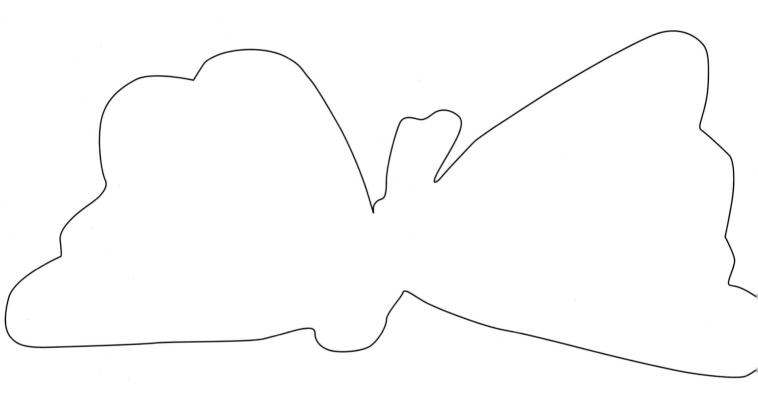

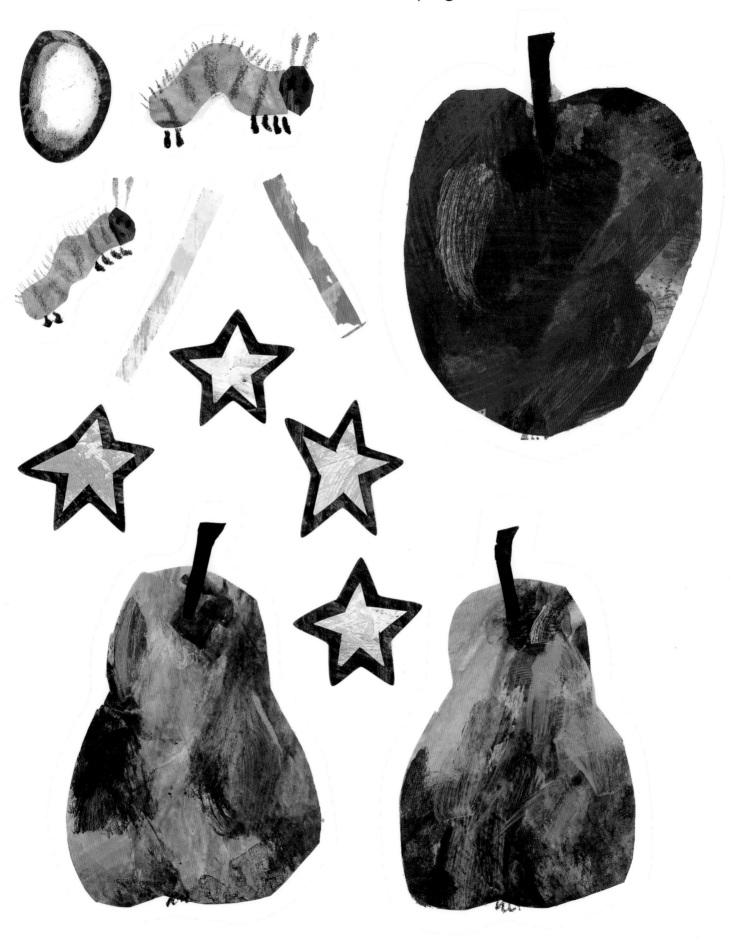

Use these stickers on pages 9–10

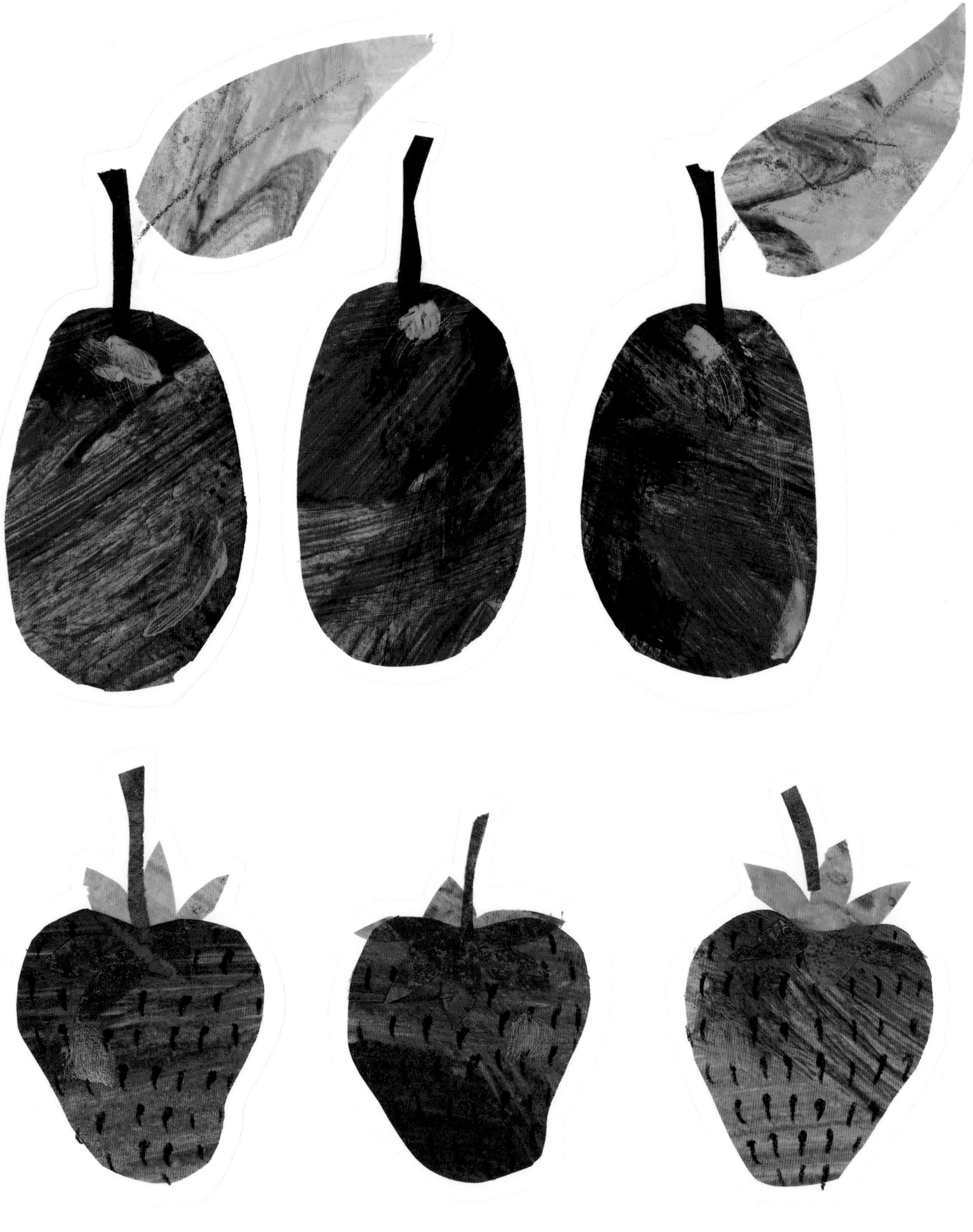

# Use these stickers on pages 10–13